NOLAN'S SHADOW

By Timothy Graf

Illustrated by i Cenizal

To James and Meghan,
Nolan is the inspiration.
Peace & love!

Introduction

One day, Nolan and his family came over for a visit to our house. We watched Nolan happy and smiling as he danced to his shadow. You see, Nolan has Coffin Siris Syndrome, a very rare Syndrome that can cause developmental delays. Nolan, the character in this book, is wearing the colors blue and yellow to represent the ribbon for this Syndrome. It is my hope that this book brings awareness to CSS, and encourages us all to take time for the gift of life and appreciate the small things. After all, those are the best things.

On a bright sunny day,
Nolan went outside to play.

With a smile on his face,
and the wind through his hair,
he thought to himself:
"My, my, what is that there?

I see a shape a lot like mine.
It seems to follow me all the time.

When I bend to touch my toes,
or stretch to reach the sky,
it's right there in front of me,
reaching just as high.

When I dance and clap my hands,
it's right there by my side.
It follows me everywhere,
especially outside.

When I travel to my friends house,
it comes along for the ride.

It will never leave me lonely,
but sometimes it will hide.

fall,

summer,

as I grow it gets so tall.

IT'S A SHADOW!

IT'S A SHADOW!

That's what it's called!

IT'S MY SHADOW,
IT'S MY SHADOW

up on the wall."

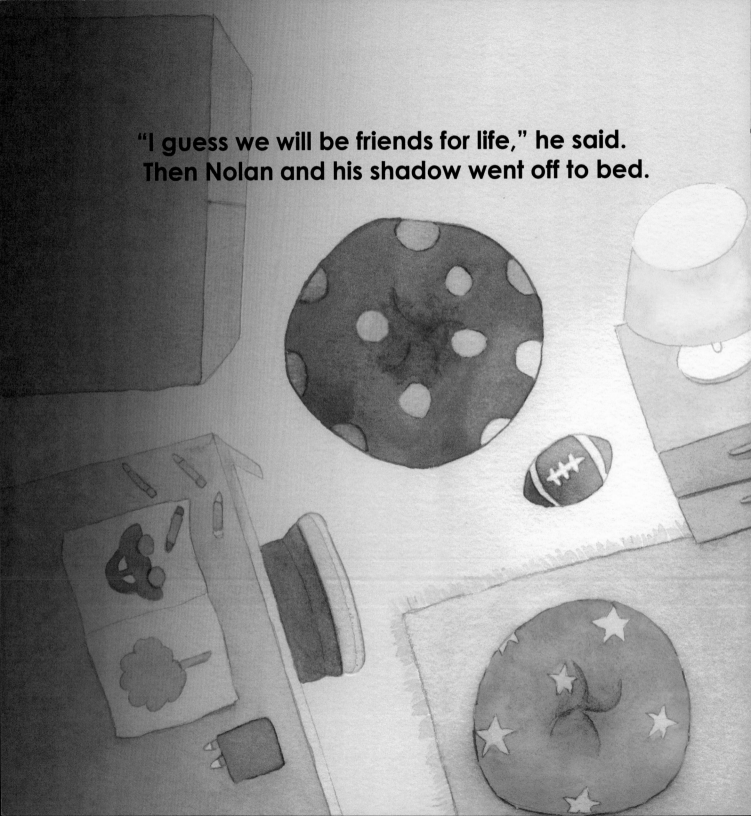

"I guess we will be friends for life," he said.
Then Nolan and his shadow went off to bed.

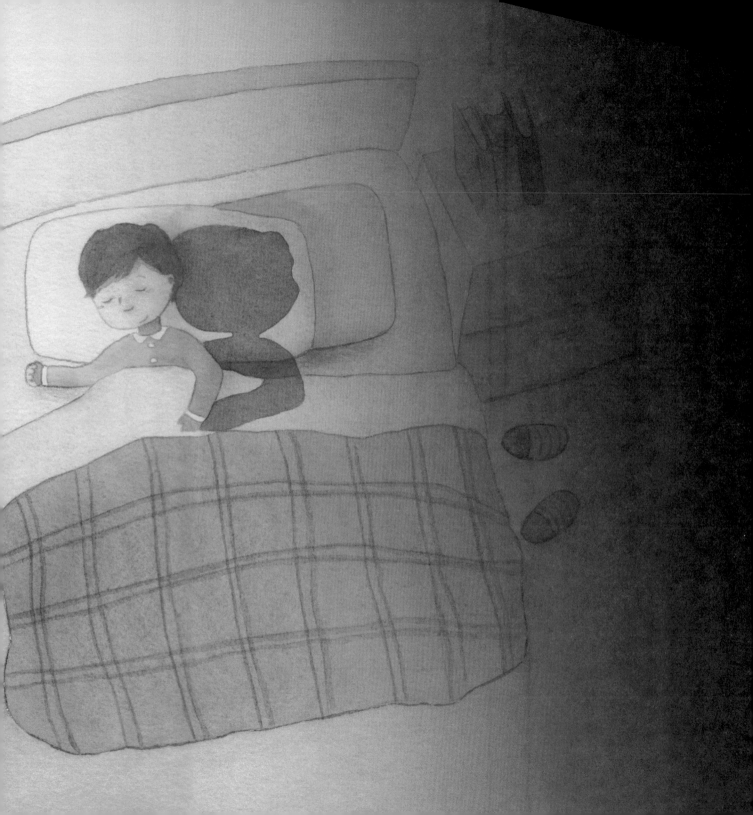

About the Author

Timothy Graf is an entrepreneur and former business owner in the healthcare space. He is living his best life on Long Island, NY along side his wife Alexis and his two boys Jack and Bear. He currently enjoys writing song lyrics and being in the great outdoors.

About the Illustrator

An honours graduate of the London Art College, *i Cenizal*
has illustrated dozens of children's books for authors
around the world. When she's not drawing for kids,
Cenizal loves to paint watercolors, many of which are on
display in a prominent gallery in Doha, Qatar,
where she currently lives.